THIS WALKER BOOK
BELONGS TO:

_____

_____

First published in *Fairy Tales* 2000 by Walker Books Ltd
87 Vauxhall Walk, London SE11 5HJ

This edition published 2010

2 4 6 8 10 9 7 5 3 1

Text © 2000 Berlie Doherty
Illustrations © 2000 Jane Ray

The right of Berlie Doherty and Jane Ray to be identified respectively
as the author and illustrator of this work has been asserted by them
in accordance with the Copyright, Designs and Patents Act 1988

This book has been typeset in Palatino

Printed in China

British Library Cataloguing in Publication Data:
a catalogue record for this book is available from the British Library

ISBN 978-1-4063-2975-9

www.walker.co.uk

Aladdin

BERLIE DOHERTY

Illustrated by

JANE RAY

WALKER BOOKS
AND SUBSIDIARIES
LONDON • BOSTON • SYDNEY

In a city in China long ago, there lived a poor widow and her only son, Aladdin.

One day a sorcerer came looking for something in that very city. He knew what it was he was looking for, but he needed someone very small and quick to get it for him. And when he saw Aladdin dodging round the bazaar and helping himself to fruit off the stalls he knew he had found exactly the right person. He pretended to be his long-lost uncle, and promised him a carpet shop if he would

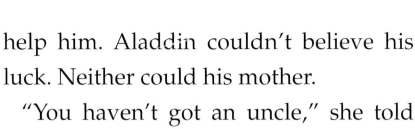

help him. Aladdin couldn't believe his luck. Neither could his mother.

"You haven't got an uncle," she told him. "But this man looks as if he's got more money than sense. Bring him in."

So, next day the sorcerer took Aladdin for a walk, and they ended up in a chrysanthemum garden. "Ah, at last!" the sorcerer sighed. "I've come all the way from Morocco to find this garden. Now you can help me."

He asked Aladdin to gather twigs and light a fire, then he threw a pinch of incense into the flames. The sky grew dark and the earth was covered with sweet smoke. And when the smoke cleared, there was a marble slab with a golden ring right in front of them. "Lift the slab," the sorcerer said. "Only you can do it."

The slab looked very heavy, and Aladdin's muscles were the size of peas, but he did as he was told, reciting his name and his mother's as he pulled, and up the slab came as if it was made of paper.

"Now," said the sorcerer, clapping his hands, "there are caves full of treasure down there. I want you to go down and walk through four caverns. Each will contain four gold chests. Don't touch them, or anything around them, or you'll be turned into stone. Go through into the fourth chamber and out into a garden of fruit trees, and through that, up some stairs, you will see a lamp hanging. Bring

it to me. You may take whatever fruit you like from the trees, but nothing else."

The sorcerer took off his ring and put it on Aladdin's finger. "This will keep you safe. You are a man now."

Fearful and proud and excited, Aladdin did as he was told. He went down into the dark cave and into a cavern with walls crusted with green emeralds, and another crusted with red rubies, and another with blue amethysts, and another with shimmering diamonds, so bright that you would think the stars had fallen out of the sky.

In each of the caverns there were chests overflowing with gold coins, but Aladdin hurried past them all, and came into a garden where the trees were loaded

down with glowing fruit. He hurried past, and climbed up the steps at the end, and there he found the lamp. There was nothing special about it, in fact it was battered and rusty, but he tucked it under his shirt.

When he came to the fruit he remembered that he could take some, but as soon as he touched them the apples and lemons and pineapples and cherries all turned into glass, every one. The colours were so rich and beautiful that he wanted to show them to his mother and he took them anyway, and stuffed them into his pockets and down his shirt and up his sleeves. He could hardly move, and when he reached the way out he couldn't climb up to it.

"Uncle, give me a hand," he called up.

"Pass the lamp up, pass the lamp up," the sorcerer hissed.

"I can't! I'm stuck! Help me out first."

Well, the sorcerer was sure that Aladdin was was trying to steal the lamp from him.

"Once a thief, always a thief!" he snarled. In a rage he slammed the slab back over Aladdin's head and sealed him underground.

Aladdin didn't know what to do with himself. He wrung his hands in despair, and by chance he rubbed the ring that the sorcerer had given him. At once there was a puff of smoke and a little fat genie appeared, sitting cross-legged about half a metre off the ground, arms folded and smiling like a cat.

"I am the genie of the ring. Tell me your wish, O Master."

"Get me out of here!" No sooner had Aladdin said it than he was back in the bazaar telling his mother about the wonderful things he had seen in the caverns. She didn't believe a word of it.

"So much fuss over a rusty old lamp," she said. "Well, the best thing I can do is sell it! Not that we'll get much for it. I'll just give it a bit of a polish and see if I can brighten it up." She rubbed it with an old cloth and *flash!* another genie appeared, pouring himself like wreaths of smoke out of the mouth of the lamp, rising higher and higher above them until he was taller than a temple. Aladdin's mother fell to her knees in fright, but by now Aladdin knew what genies could do.

"What is your wish, O Master?" the genie asked, in a voice that rumbled like the heart of a volcano.

"Slave of the lamp," Aladdin said, as if he was the sultan himself, "fetch us some food."

Puff! The genie disappeared. A flash or two later he was back with a silver tray loaded with so many plates of food that Aladdin and his mother didn't stop eating for a month. Then Aladdin sold the silver plates and, after that, the tray, and he and his mother were better off than they had ever been in their lives.

But then, something even more wonderful happened to Aladdin. He fell in love. It was quite easy to see that this had happened because he stopped eating or sleeping and mooned round the bazaar singing and sighing until at last his mother said, "Tell me who she is, Aladdin. This girl who's stolen your heart away. Who is she?"

"The sultan's daughter," he said gloomily. "The beautiful Princess Badr-al-Budur! I thought all women looked like you, Mother, but now I've seen her I know what real beauty is."

"Well!" gasped his mother. "What a thing to say!"

"I want to marry her, Mother."

"Marry the sultan's daughter! Are you mad! He'll have your head for a cannon ball if you ask him to give you his daughter."

"That's why I want you to ask him for me," Aladdin said. "But what gifts can I send?"

And then he remembered the glass fruits that he had brought from the cave. As he unwrapped them they saw them for what they really were – not glass at all, but rubies and diamonds, topaz, emeralds, amethyst, all glittering and sparkling and flashing like fishes in a stream.

"Take these to the sultan," Aladdin begged his mother. "And ask if I can marry the Princess Badr-al-Budur."

And his mother did. She had to go to the golden palace every day for a week, and queue up with all the other people who had brought gifts, but at last the sultan agreed to see her. He was so impressed with her wealth that he agreed that his daughter would marry Aladdin in three months' time. Aladdin's mother rushed home and danced all round the bazaar with her son.

But the sultan didn't keep his word. A month later the Princess Badr-al-Budur was married to the son of the sultan's grand-vizier. Aladdin was mad with despair. He snatched up his enchanted lamp and rubbed it and *flash!* up billowed the genie in a cloud of green smoke.

"What is your wish, O Master?" he rumbled, bowing to the ground.

"Bring me the princess and that soppy-faced husband of hers!" Aladdin ordered, and it was done. No sooner had the princess and the son of the grand-vizier climbed into bed for the night than the bed whizzed out of the window and over the town and landed in Aladdin's

house. He threw the grand-vizier's son out on to the dung heap. This happened night after night, until at last the princess and the grand-vizier's son were so fed up with this treatment that they decided the marriage was definitely off. And next day, Aladdin's mother was knocking at the palace door demanding to see the sultan.

"You promised the princess to my son," she reminded him.

"Ah, so I did," said the sultan. "Well, it looks as if she isn't married after all. Tell your son that if he can bring me forty times the jewels he brought before, with forty slaves and forty slave-girls to carry them, he can marry my daughter."

Aladdin's mother trudged home with

the news. "I wish you'd never clapped eyes on that princess," she said. "Where are you going to get that lot from, Aladdin?"

He picked up his enchanted lamp and rubbed it, and *flash!* up flowed the genie, bowing low.

"What is your wish, O Master?"

Before Aladdin's mother had time to tidy up the house, it was full of slaves and slave-girls staggering under the weight of their trays of jewels. She led them off to the palace at once, and this time the sultan welcomed her with open arms. She ran home to Aladdin, and they danced round the bazaar and all the way up to the palace, with more slaves and jewels sent up by the helpful genie.

The sultan himself came out to meet them and flung his arms round Aladdin.

"What a splendid son-in-law you'll make! Of course you can marry my daughter! Why didn't you ask me before?"

But Aladdin had a request to make. "I can't marry your daughter until I have built a beautiful palace for her," he said. "May I have this plot of land just in front of yours?"

"Of course. But won't it take a little time?"

"Leave it to me," said Aladdin. When he got home he rubbed his enchanted lamp and called up the genie, and during the night the most exquisite palace sprang up, as golden as the sun itself and

glittering with jewels that were every colour of the rainbow. The sultan's palace looked quite small behind it.

"Wonderful!" breathed the sultan, gazing at it out of his window. "How on earth did he do it?"

"By magic," his grand-vizier said. "Only magic could do this. Believe me."

So the Princess Badr-al-Budur and Aladdin were married at last, and they moved into the shimmering palace with Aladdin's mother, and were very happy.

But that isn't the end of the story.

Far away in Morocco the sorcerer heard about the wonderful palace that had sprung up as if by magic, and he came to China to look at it. As soon as he knew that Aladdin was living in it he guessed what had happened. He disguised himself as an old man and had some lamps made, and went round the streets calling out the strangest thing: "New lamps for old! New lamps for old!" Everyone thought he was mad. The princess heard him and sent her maid to fetch him in.

"Give him that rusty old lamp of Aladdin's!" she said. "I'll surprise him with a nice new one."

But there was no time for that. As soon as the maid came out with the lamp, the sorcerer snatched it out of her hands and rubbed it. *Flash!* the genie appeared. "What is your wish, O Master?"

"Take me and this palace and the princess to Morocco right away."

And it was no sooner said than done. The palace and the princess disappeared as if they had never been, and the sultan was furious. He sent his guards out to find Aladdin and flung him and his mother into prison.

"Now see what you've done," his mother moaned, but the sultan's anger was even greater.

"I've had enough of your magic tricks! Find my daughter, or I'll throw your head on the dung heap. *And* your mother's."

So Aladdin was freed for forty days, but he had no idea what to do or where to look. He went to wash himself in a stream so he could think clearly, and as he wrung his hands together he rubbed his ring. Suddenly, *puff!* a cloud of smoke, and the forgotten fat little genie of the ring appeared.

"What is your wish, O Master?"

Aladdin could have wept for joy. "Take me to my wife," he begged. "That's all I want."

The genie stroked his wispy beard. "I can get you there, but I can't get you back," he said. "It'll use up all my magic as it is."

Aladdin found himself being lifted up and floated over the temples and mountains of China, and over the blue of the oceans, and over the golden deserts of Africa, and at last he was in the arms of his princess.

"Tell me where my lamp is," he asked

her, "and we can go back home."

"Your lamp! But I gave it to the maid, and she gave it to the old man. He's the one who brought me here."

Aladdin knew at once who it must be. The sorcerer was fast asleep, snoring away in Aladdin's own bed. Aladdin crept up to him and stole the lamp from inside his shirt, rubbed it quickly, and *flash!* there was his genie, towering over him and bowing to the ground.

"Take us home!" Aladdin asked him. "O wonderful genie, take us home!"

Puff! The palace was returned to China. Aladdin gave the sultan the sorcerer's head instead of his own, the sultan embraced his daughter and his son-in-law, Aladdin's mother was released from prison, and they all lived in great happiness until the day they died.

And that *is* the end of the story.

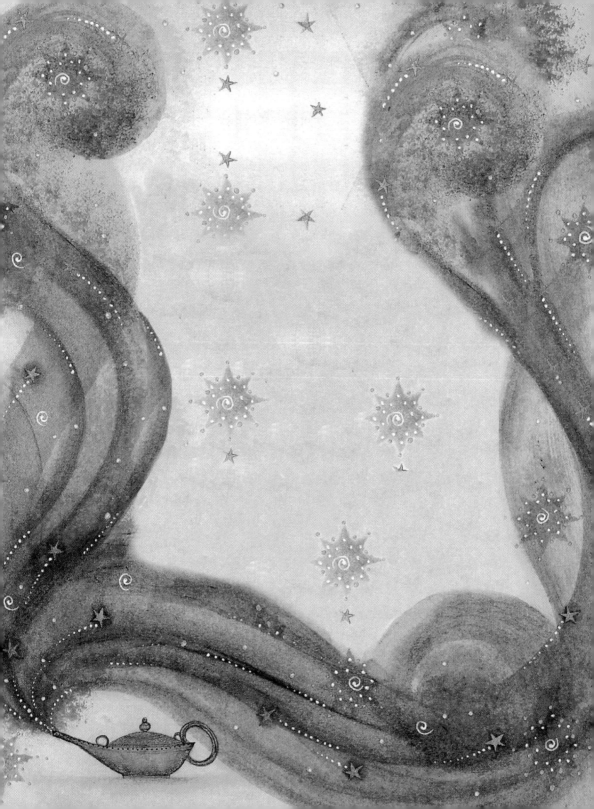

TITLES IN THE FAIRY TALE SERIES

Available from all good bookstores

www.walker.co.uk

FOR THE BEST CHILDREN'S BOOKS, LOOK FOR THE BEAR.